TURKEY RIDDLES

by Katy Hall and Lisa Eisenberg

pictures by Kristin Sorra

PUFFIN BOOKS

PUFFIN BOOKS
Published by the Penguin Group
Penguin Young Readers Group, 345 Hudson Street, New York, New York 10014, U.S.A.
Penguin Group (Canada), 10 Alcorn Avenue, Toronto, Ontario, Canada M4V 3B2
(a division of Pearson Penguin Canada Inc.)
Penguin Books Ltd, 80 Strand, London WC2R 0RL, England
Penguin Ireland, 25 St Stephen's Green, Dublin 2, Ireland (a division of Penguin Books Ltd)
Penguin Group (Australia), 250 Camberwell Road, Camberwell, Victoria 3124,
Australia (a division of Pearson Australia Group Pty Ltd)
Penguin Books India Pvt Ltd, 11 Community Centre, Panchsheel Park,
New Delhi - 110 017, India
Penguin Group (NZ), Cnr Airborne and Rosedale Roads, Albany, Auckland 1310,
New Zealand (a division of Pearson New Zealand Ltd)
Penguin Books (South Africa) (Pty) Ltd, 24 Sturdee Avenue, Rosebank,
Johannesburg 2196, South Africa

Registered Offices: Penguin Books Ltd, 80 Strand, London WC2R 0RL, England

First published in the United States of America by Dial Books for
Young Readers, a division of Penguin Putnam Inc., 2002
Published by Puffin Books, a division of Penguin Young Readers Group, 2005

3 5 7 9 10 8 6 4

Text copyright © Kate McMullan and Lisa Eisenberg, 2002
Pictures copyright © Kristin Sorra, 2002
All rights reserved

THE LIBRARY OF CONGRESS HAS CATALOGED THE DIAL BOOKS
FOR YOUNG READERS EDITION AS FOLLOWS:
Hall, Katy.
Turkey riddles/by Katy Hall and Lisa Eisenberg; pictures by Kristin Sorra.
p. cm.
Summary: A collection of nearly three dozen riddles featuring turkeys, such as
"What happened when Tom Turkey stepped up to the plate? He hit a fowl ball."
ISBN: 0-8037-2530-2 (hc)
1. Riddles, Juvenile. 2. Turkeys—Juvenile humor.
[1. Turkeys—Humor. 2. Riddles. 3. Jokes.]
I. Sorra, Kristin, ill. II. Title.
PN6371.5.H379 2002 398.6—dc21 2001047475

Puffin Books ISBN 0-14-240369-5

Puffin® and Easy-to-Read® are registered trademarks of Penguin Group (USA) Inc.

Manufactured in China

The art was drawn with pen and ink, then scanned and colored in Photoshop.

Reading Level 2.4

*For Mrs. Arth and all the great riddlers
at Alexander Doniphan School*

K.H.

To all the turkeys I've known in my life

L.E.

To Neil Jr.

K.S.

What happened to the turkey
who ate too much corn?

He got an ear-ache.

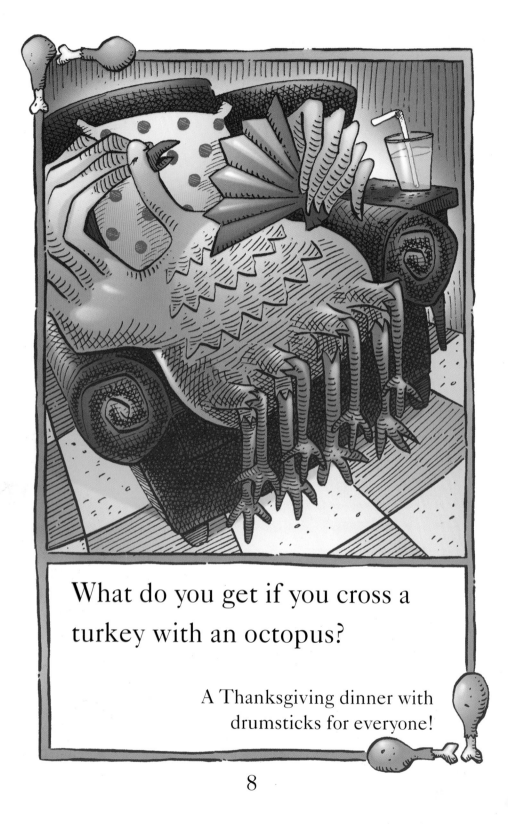

What do you get if you cross a turkey with an octopus?

A Thanksgiving dinner with drumsticks for everyone!

What did the papa turkey say to the little turkey at supper time?

"Must you gobble, gobble, gobble your food?"

What did the vampire say to
the turkey?

"Happy Fangs-giving!"

What costume did the little turkey wear every Halloween?

He was always a-gobblin'.

Why did the stuffing hide
behind the turkey?

It was dressing.

What happened when Tom Turkey stepped up to the plate?

He hit a fowl ball.

What is Superturkey's real name?

Cluck Kent.

What do you call a gobbler in a flowered shirt, plaid shorts, and a beanie?

A *real* turkey!

What did the sweet potato say
to the turkey?

"Here I yam!"

How is a penny like a turkey sitting on a fence?

Head's on one side, and tail's on the other!

What happened when the fairy godmother waved her wand at the turkey?

She granted her wishbone.

What did the turkey say when the Pilgrim passed the potatoes?

"No, thanks. I'm stuffed."

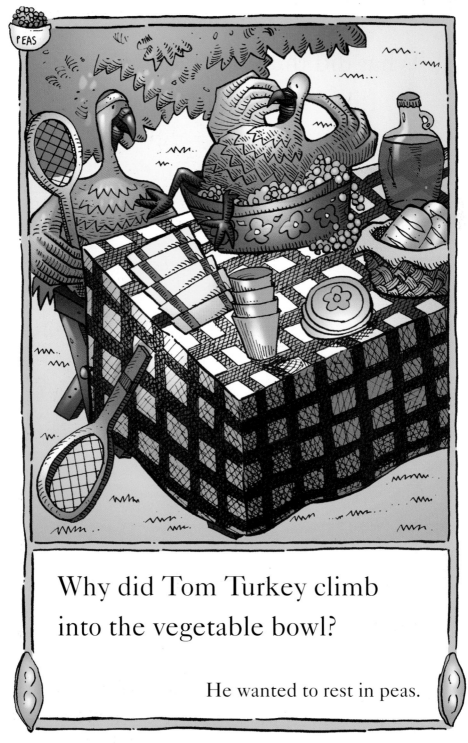

Why did Tom Turkey climb
into the vegetable bowl?

He wanted to rest in peas.

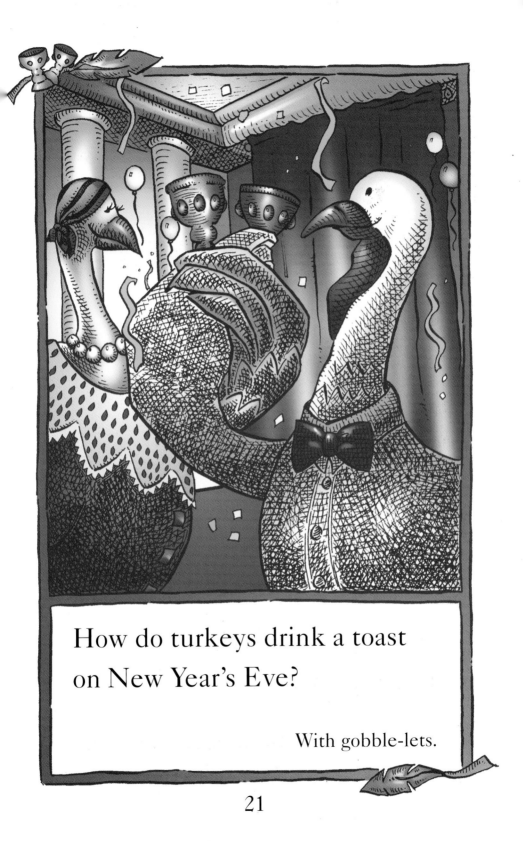

How do turkeys drink a toast
on New Year's Eve?

With gobble-lets.

Why did the turkey stuffing go on strike?

It wanted a higher celery!

What did the little turkey
say when he brought his dad
breakfast in bed?

"Happy Feather's Day!"

Why did the silly pig cover his ears when he passed the turkeys?

He didn't want to hear any fowl language.

How did the cook get locked out of the kitchen?

All the tur-*keys* were inside.

What do you get if you cross a turkey with a bottle of glue?

Gobbledy-gook!

Do turkeys dance cheek to cheek?

No, beak to beak.

What's the difference between a turkey and an owl?

A turkey doesn't give a hoot.

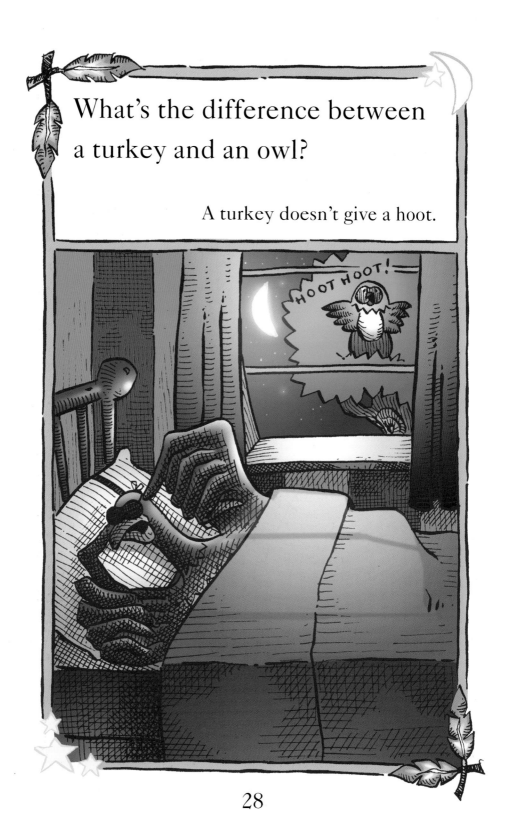

What do turkeys sing when at birthday parties?

"Happy Bird-day to You!"

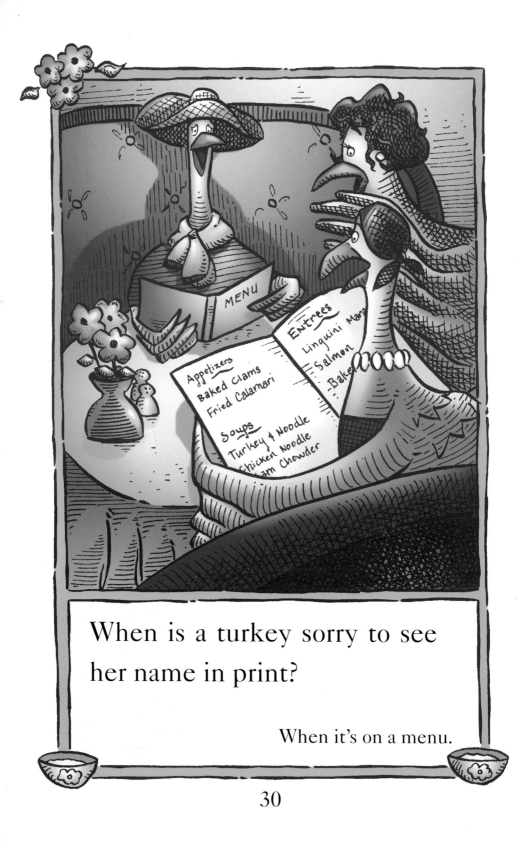

When is a turkey sorry to see her name in print?

When it's on a menu.

Why did the smart turkey carry an umbrella to work?

She'd watched the evening feather report!

What is a turkey's favorite day
to celebrate?

The day *after* Thanksgiving.

What did the turkey waiter say
to his customers?

"Wattle it be, folks?"

What do you call a turkey who cleans his house all day?

A feather duster!

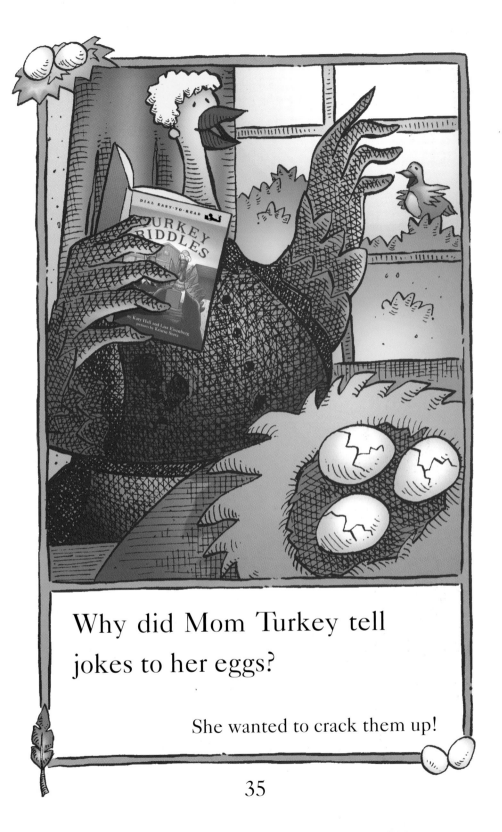

Why did Mom Turkey tell jokes to her eggs?

She wanted to crack them up!

Why isn't it safe for turkeys to do math?

If they add 3 and 5, they get ate!

What movie do little turkeys like to watch?

The Gizzard of Oz.

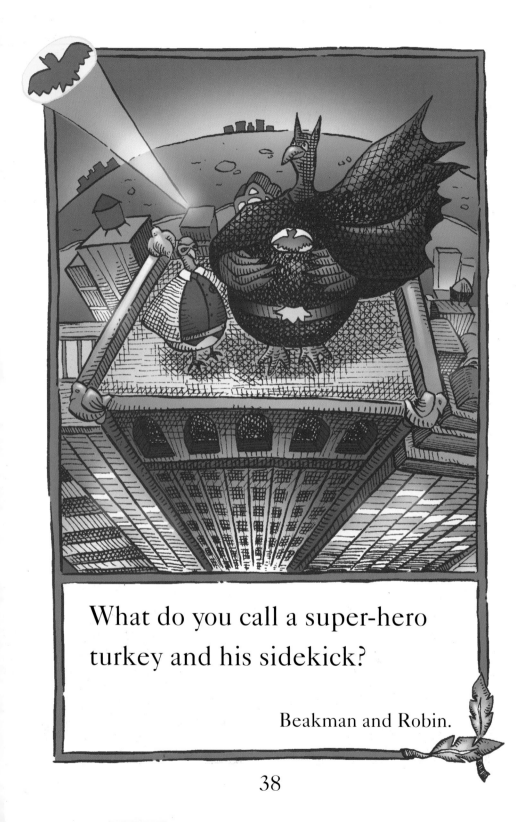

What do you call a super-hero
turkey and his sidekick?

Beakman and Robin.

Why did the silly cat put her turkey in a ball gown?

She heard you were supposed to dress a turkey.

What's made of turkey and rice, comes in a can, and wears a cape?

Turkey Soup-erman!